FINISH STRONG

SEVEN
Marathons,
SEVEN
Continents,
SEVEN
Days

Dave McGillivray
Boston Marathon Race Director

with Nancy Feehrer

Illustrated by Shululu

Dedication

This book is lovingly dedicated to heart warriors everywhere.

And to Katie McGillivray and John Feehrer: patient, encouraging partners who have cheered us on to finish strong!

A portion of the proceeds from this book will go to the
Joseph Middlemiss Big Heart Foundation (jmbigheart.org).

Acknowledgments

A huge and heart-felt thank you to the *Joseph Middlemiss Big Heart Foundation* and Scott and Kate Middlemiss for their partnership in spreading kindness and inspiration to thousands of children.

Thanks to our official readers for offering advice and edits over the course of three books and countless drafts. *Patience is a virtue . . . and a pain!*

Team Hold the Plane! Thanks for your friendship and encouragement: Deb Carneol, Josh Cohen, Jeff Conine, Michael Hill, Sarah Lacina, P.J. Loyello, Brad Miller, Mitch Moser, Cara Nelson, Bret Parker, Sarah Reinertsen, David Samson, Josh Samson, Judy Sanchez, John Silverman, and Mikayla Wingle.

David Samson invited me to join in on this extraordinary worldwide adventure. Many thanks for the journey of a lifetime! Thanks also to Richard Donovan, founder and race director of the World Marathon Challenge.

Special thanks to Becca Pizzi and Michael Wardian for their training tips and constant encouragement. Truly appreciated!

Nomad Press
A division of Nomad Communications
10 9 8 7 6 5 4 3 2 1

This book was manufactured by CGB Printers,
North Mankato, Minnesota, United States
March 2021, Job #1018003

ISBN: 978-1-64741-039-1

Questions regarding the ordering of this book should be addressed to

Nomad Press
2456 Christian St.
White River Junction, VT 05001

www.nomadpress.net

Printed in the United States.

When I was a kid, I loved sports—baseball, basketball, football.
But I was small. Because of my size, no one would give me a chance.

**I was always picked on,
picked last,
or not picked at all.**

So, at age 12, I turned to running.
No one can stop you from running—*you just . . . RUN!*

Set goals, not limits.

Since then, I've done many challenging runs:

running my age in miles on my birthdays,

running 3,452 miles across America in 80 days,

running for 24 hours straight,

running a marathon blindfolded,

running from Florida to Massachusetts with a friend in a wheelchair—

and all of it for charity.

Your greatest accomplishment is your next one.

One day, a friend called and invited me to run the *World Marathon Challenge.*

7 marathons
on 7 continents
in 7 days

Was that even possible?

We started training and called ourselves "Team Hold the Plane!" We learned that for the first marathon, we'd be running in a desert. You're probably thinking sand, heat, and cactuses. But, actually, we'd be starting in Antarctica!

The world is full of surprises.

Antarctica, as it turns out, is the
icy-est,
   windy-est,
      dry-est continent.

Because it's so cold, it rarely rains or snows—so, it's considered a desert. *Who knew?!?*

I was nervous about the plane landing on **ICE**. Would it crack? Fortunately, the ice on Antarctica can be up to **3 miles thick!** *Phew!*

After we landed, we were taken to a pod to rest and change.

In Antarctica, the permanent "people" population is exactly zero.
No one lives there year-round.

But the penguin population? That's a different story.

There are more than 12 million penguins.

(That was good, because if I got lost, I might need to ask
for directions!)

It takes more guts to get to the
starting line than to the finish line.

"On your mark, get set, go!"

Off we ran for our first marathon! Cold, fresh air filled my lungs and little white clouds puffed from my mouth. My feet crunched with each icy stride.

"Hey! Wait a minute!" Crunch, crunch, crunch. "Why aren't we going to run on the earth's other big chunk of ice? If Antarctica is a continent, why isn't the Arctic a continent?" (You have a lot of time to think when you're running a marathon on ice.)

I later found out that the Arctic is an <u>ocean</u> with a thick sheet of ice *floating* on it.

Antarctica has <u>land</u> underneath.

26.2 cold, crunchy miles later, I had finished the first marathon!

I went to the pod and ate mashed potatoes and a hot dog—not what I usually eat, but, boy, they tasted good.

We boarded the plane at 11 p.m., heading for Africa.

From the freezer to the furnace!

Well begun is half done.
Well . . . almost.

Cape Town was hot—about 80 degrees—and the landscape couldn't have been more different from Antarctica. Here, it was
colorful,
      lush, and
            full of life.
For this marathon, we ran loops along the South Atlantic Ocean—

lots and lots of loops!

When you run, it's important to stay hydrated. In Africa, they gave us water in small blue packets.

We quickly learned the schedule for this marathon challenge:

1. **Fly, eat, and <u>try</u> to sleep**

2. **Land**

3. **RUN!**

4. **Repeat (<u>seven times</u>)**

Whenever the plane landed, that's when we had to run a marathon—and I mean *whenever*.

Two o'clock in the morning? Yep!

Hop off the plane, run 26.2 miles, get back on the plane, and fly to the next continent. That's exactly what I did after the marathon in Africa. Now, time to fly to the world's *smallest* continent!

Haste makes waste . . . unless you are running around the world.

Our next marathon was in Australia. It was a long flight from Cape Town to Perth. **Twelve hours, to be exact.**

We landed and walked to the starting point near a stadium.

The only trouble was . . . **CRICKET!**

Not cricket the bug, but cricket the sport.

There was a cricket match going on near the marathon course.
We had to wait until the match ended to begin our run.

Cricket is similar to baseball, but it's played with a flat
bat and the players run back and forth on a strip
of grass instead of around bases.

Patience is a virtue . . . and a pain.

Finally, late at night, we began our run.

The marathon course went back and forth along a path—kind of like cricket!

The best part was that with each pass, I could see all my new friends.

"Keep going!"
"You can do it!"
"G'day, mate!"

Since we didn't start running until 11 p.m., we didn't finish until 4 a.m. Three marathons? Done!

My legs? They were DONE, too!

Next stop: The *biggest* continent in the world.

Friends make the journey joyful.

More than *half* of the world's people live in Asia.

The United Arab Emirates is in a part of Asia called the Middle East. It's **hot**, **dry**, and **sandy**. But rising up out of the sandy landscape is an incredible, modern city called Dubai.

I was surprised to learn that Dubai has an *indoor* snow ski resort at a mall.

"Hey! I could eat at the food court, buy a new pair of sneakers, and ski all in one place!"

On the way to the marathon starting point, our bus driver got lost, and it took more than an hour to drive just a few miles.

We could have run there faster than that!

When we finally began our marathon, it was 26.2 miles of out-and-back loops along the Persian Gulf.

My running time in Asia was about four and a half hours. In twice that amount of time, I'd be running my next marathon . . . in Europe.

Never underestimate your own abilities.

We landed in Lisbon in a chilly drizzle and started our fifth marathon at night.

Click! Slap! Clunk! Smack!

Those were the sounds of my sneakers running on cobblestone, cement, wooden docks, and asphalt—each step producing a different sound and feel. My legs hurt, and all these different surfaces didn't help.

16

Part of this marathon took us through a busy outdoor market. We had to weave in and out of the surprised shoppers!

Did they think we stole something?

If so, no one stopped us. They just gave us confused looks and stepped aside.

Portugal was lively, colorful, and cold! I was looking forward to our next run in sunny South America.

When in doubt, step aside.

We started our second-to-last marathon in the center of
Cartagena's old city.

It was hot, hot, HOT!

We ran in streets crowded with people, bikes, buses, horse-drawn
wagons, cars, and motorcycles.

18

During the race, my left leg really started to hurt. I saw our medical doctor on one of the laps and asked for help.

As I continued to run, I prayed that I would get through this race. There was only *one more marathon* to go, and that one was back home.

My friends ran alongside to encourage and support me. With their help, I finished the sixth marathon. **But my leg was killing me.**

Finish strong?
I wondered if I'd finish at all.

Ask for help when you need it.
Give help whenever you can.

Exhausted and in pain, we arrived in the USA to a hero's welcome!

Were we heroes? Survivors? Or just crazy?

Everyone on our trip was running for a purpose, and most had raised money for charity. So, maybe the answer was *all three.*

We were enjoying the celebration until we remembered: **We still had one more marathon to run!**

And I was sick. The medicine the doctor had given me for my leg made my stomach hurt. It was hot in Miami, too, and I worried that I wouldn't make it to the end.

Once again, my friends came to the rescue!

They shouted encouragement each lap until I crossed the finish line.

DAVE KEEP GOING!

GO DAVE!

You don't just "get by" with a little help from your friends. You thrive.

And guess what? My last 10 miles were the *fastest* I'd run all week.

7 marathons on
7 continents in
7 days:
DONE!

I gave it everything I had and finished the World Marathon Challenge. What did I get—besides seven medals and very sore legs?

Did you know that although Australia is the *smallest* continent, it's the *biggest* island in the world?

This reminded me . . . of me!

You don't have to be the biggest or the best at *everything*. You can still finish strong at *something*.

It just takes big dreams, hard work, and great friends.

Finish strong . . . or weak.
Just finish!

#5 LISBON Portugal

#7 MIAMI Florida

#6 CARTAGENA Colombia

#4 **DUBAI** United Arab Emirates

#3 **PERTH** Australia

#2 **CAPE TOWN** South Africa

#1 **NOVO** Antarctica

25

Dear Friends,

Thank you for reading about my journey around the world! I hope that someday you can work hard to make your big dreams come true.

This story didn't end when I finished the World Marathon Challenge.

After I came home, I noticed that I had a little trouble breathing when I ran. I figured I was just recovering from my 7-7-7 adventure.

But then . . .

I went to my doctor and he said that I had a big problem with my heart. At first, I was embarrassed. "Hey! I just ran around the world! My heart must be fine!"

But, it wasn't.

I needed surgery to fix it.

If you feel something, say something.

I discovered that you can't change what you are born with. That's the bad news.

The good news is this: You can change your behavior.

Here's what I do to help my heart:

- Eat more fruits and vegetables.
- Get more sleep.
- Exercise, but also relax!

You can do these things, too, to take care of your heart.

Remember: DREAM BIG, WORK HARD, AND FINISH STRONG!

—Dave McGillivray

Just because you're fit,
doesn't mean you're healthy.

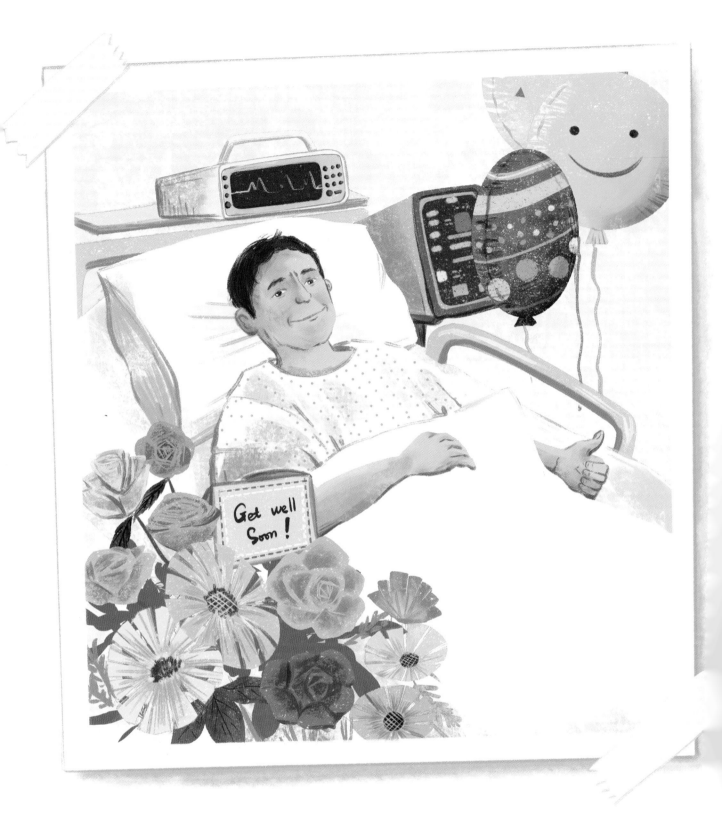

The comeback is always
stronger than the setback.

Dave gave all his World Marathon Challenge medals to his hero and heart-warrior buddy, 5-year-old Jack! Jack had a heart transplant the same year Dave ran the World Marathon Challenge.

A year later, Jack gave a medal to his friend Dave after Dave finished the Boston Marathon—just six months after having heart surgery.

The DREAM BIG "Marathon"

To make your **BIG DREAMS** come true, you need to **BE FIT**—physically, mentally, and emotionally. Challenge yourself to **run** 26 miles, **read** 26 books, and **do** 26 acts of kindness in 26 weeks!

RUN! 26 MILES

Try running or walking just a mile at a time. Go to **DreamBigWithDave.org** to get started. There, you can download a printable sheet to keep track of your 26-week challenge. Check with your doctor first to make sure you're healthy and then *get moving*!

READ! 26 BOOKS

For ideas on great books for any age or interest, go to **Scholastic.com**. Just learning to read? Have an adult read to you. Reading chapter books? Aim for 10 pages a day or about 70 pages a week.

REACH OUT!
26 ACTS OF BIG-HEARTED KINDNESS

For a list of creative acts of kindness, check out the Joseph Middlemiss Big Heart Foundation at **JMBigHeart.org**. While you're there, read about Joseph's story and the amazing acts of kindness the Big Heart Foundation does.

THE FINISH LINE!

Go to **DreamBigWithDave.org** to find out how to get your very own *Dream Big "Marathon" Race Medal** for making it to the finish line!

*while supplies last

The **Dream Big Marathon** is modeled on the **GO! St. Louis Read, Right, and Run Marathon™**. Credit for the fantastic idea and special thanks to Nancy Lieberman and the **GO! St. Louis Marathon**.